# ·→ ‖ ACKNOWLEDGEMENTS ‖ ←·

The publishers would like to thank the following sources for permission to reproduce their pictures:

FINE ART PHOTOGRAPHS & LIBRARY LTD: pages 11, 13, 14, 17, 25, 29, 30, 41, 43, 46, 55, 56, 59, 65, 66, 72, 79, 80, 85, 86, 93, 96, 100, 102, 105, 108, 113, 114, 116, 119, 121, 122, 125

E.T. ARCHIVE: pages 18, 21, 23, 35, 38, 48, 49, 68, 88, 91, 94, 111

THE BRIDGEMAN ART LIBRARY: pages 45, 76, 99, 106

THE CHRIS BEETLES GALLERY, LONDON: pages 8, 22, 26, 36, 51, 52, 60, 71, 75, 110

THE MARY EVANS PICTURE LIBRARY: pages 10, 64

The publishers would also like to acknowledge the following writers and poets:

p.8 THOMAS LOVELL BEDDOES (1803–1849) *Song, Torrismond*
p.9 W. SOMERSET MAUGHAM (1874–1965) *The Summing Up*
p.10 ELIZABETH TOLLET (1694–1754) *Winter Song*
p.12 WILLIAM SHAKESPEARE (1564–1616)
p.13 ALICE WALKER (b.1944)
p.15 THOMAS PAINE (1737–1809)
p.16 ANTOINE DE SAINT-EXUPÉRY (1900–1944) *The Little Prince*
p.18 JOHN DRYDEN (1631–1700) *Secret-Love or The Maiden Queen*
p.19 HELEN KELLER (1880–1968)
p.20 EDMUND WALLER (1608–1687) *Go Lovely Rose*
p.22 JOHN CLARE (1793–1864) *First Love*
p.23 JUAN RUIZ DE ALARCÓN MENDOZA (c.1283–c.1350) *El Amor*
p.25 THOMAS CAMPBELL (1777–1844)
p.26 WILLIAM WORDSWORTH (1770–1850)
p.27 MAXIM GORKY (1868–1936) *The Zykovs*
p.31 SIR PHILIP SIDNEY (1554–1586) *The Bargain*
p.33 ROBERT HERRICK (1591–1674) *The Shoe Tying*
p.34 PAUL GÉRALDY (b.1885) *l'Homme et l'Amour*
p.36 RABINDRANATH TAGORE (1861–1941) *Fruit Gathering*
p.37 WILLIAM SHAKESPEARE (1564–1616) *As You Like It*
p.39 DECIMUS JUNIUS JUVENAL SATIRES(c.60–140 A.D.)
p.41 JOHN KEBLE (1792–1866) *The Christian Year*
p.43 ROBERT HERRICK (1591–1674) *The Primrose*
p.44 SAMUEL TAYLOR COLERIDGE (1772–1834)
p.45 THOMAS CAREW (1598–1638) *Celia Singing*
p.46 WILLIAM WORDSWORTH (1770–1850) *She was a Phantom of Delight*
p.47 SAMUEL BUTLER (1612–80)
p.49 LAWRENCE HOPE (1865–1904) *Carpe Diem*
p.50 GEOFFREY CHAUCER (1340–1400) *The Romaunt of the Rose*
p.53 PERCY BYSSHE SHELLEY (1792–1822)
p.55 WILLIAM CAVENDISH (1592–1676) *Love Play*

p.56 ROBERT BROWNING (1812–1889) *You'll Love Me Yet*
p.57 ROBERT BURNS (1759–1796) *O my Love is like a Red, Red Rose*
p.58 JOHN KEATS (1795–1821) *A Thing of Beauty from "Endymion"*
p.61 THOMAS OTWAY (1652–1685) *Captive*
p.62 WILLIAM SHAKESPEARE (1564–1616) *A Midsummer Night's Dream*
p.63 KAHLIL GIBRAN (1883–1931)
p.64 THOMAS LOVELL BEDDOES (1803–1849) *The Reason Why*
p.66 WILLIAM SHAKESPEARE (1564–1616) *Sonnet*
p.67 JOHANN WOLFGANG GOETHE (1749–1832) *Elective Affinities*
p.69 THOMAS CAMPION (1567–1620) *Never Love*
p.71 WILLIAM BLAKE (1757–1827) *Love's Secret*
p.73 JAPANESE LYRIC
p.74 HENRY WADSWORTH LONGFELLOW (1807–1882)
p.76 PERCY BYSSHE SHELLEY (1792–1822) *Love's Philosophy*
p.77 MARK TWAIN (1835–1910)
p.78 ALGERNON SWINBURNE (1837–1909)
p.81 ANON *To His Love*
p.82 CHRISTINA ROSSETTI (1830–1894) *Echo*
p.83 JOHN FREEMAN (1880–1929) *Nearness*
p.84 ARTHUR SYMONS (1865–1945) *Memory*
p.86 ALFRED EDWARD HOUSMAN (1859–1936) *Tell Me Not Here*
p.87 WILLIAM BLAKE (1757–1827)
p.89 EMILY DICKINSON (1830–1886) *Love Poems*
p.91 ANNE MORROW LINDBERGH (b.1906) *Second Sowing*
p.92 JOHN DRYDEN (1631–1700) *Amphitryon*
p.95 SARAH WILLIAMS (1841–68) *The Offering of the Heart*
p.96 THOMAS WOLFE (1900–1938) *Of Time and the River*
p.97 CHRISTINA ROSSETTI (1830–1894) *Remember*
p.98 THOMAS MOORE (1779–1852) *The Silent Voice*
p.101 RAINER MARIA RILKE (1875–1926) *Letters to a Young Poet*
p.102 NATHANIAL HAWTHORNE (1804–1864) *American Note-Books*
p.104 WILLIAM WORDSWORTH (1770–1850) *Why Art Thou Silent*
p.106 GEORGE GORDON BYRON (1788–1824) *She Walks in Beauty*
p.107 WILLIAM BLAKE (1757–1827) *The Smile*
p.109 STENDHAL (1783–1842) *On Love*
p.110 SIR WALTER SCOTT (1771–1832) *The Lay of the Last Minstrel*
p.113 JACQUES MARITAIN (1882–1973)
p.115 RABINDRANATH TAGORE (1861–1941) *Fruit Gathering*
p.116 JOHN KEATS (1795–1821) *In a Drear-Nighted December*
p.118 EDGAR ALLAN POE (1809–1849) *To One in Paradise*
p.121 WYSTAN HUGH AUDEN (1907–1973) *Notes on the Comic, The Dyer's Hand*
p.123 JOHN DRYDEN (1621–1700) *Ah, How Sweet it is to Love*
p.124 BLAISE PASCAL (1623–62)

THE LOVERS' BOOK OF DAYS
*Designed and produced by* THE BRIDGEWATER BOOK CO. LTD
*Compiled by* Rhoda Nottridge
*Edited by* Joanne Jessop
*Designed by* Peter Bridgewater
*Picture Research by* Felicity Cox
*Typesetting by* Vanessa Good/Chris Lanaway

CLB 3229

© 1993 Colour Library Books Ltd., Godalming, Surrey, England.
All rights reserved.
Colour separations by Scantrans Pte Ltd., Singapore.
Printed in Italy.
ISBN 1 85833 021 1

A GIFT OF DEVOTION TO

. . . . . . . . . . . . . . . . . . . . . . . . . . . . . . . . . . . .

WITH LOVE FROM

. . . . . . . . . . . . . . . . . . . . . . . . . . . . . . . . . . . .

Colour Library Books

# THE LOVERS'

### ⇥ BOOK OF DAYS ⇤

### A *Romantic Book of Days* for *Lovers* everywhere

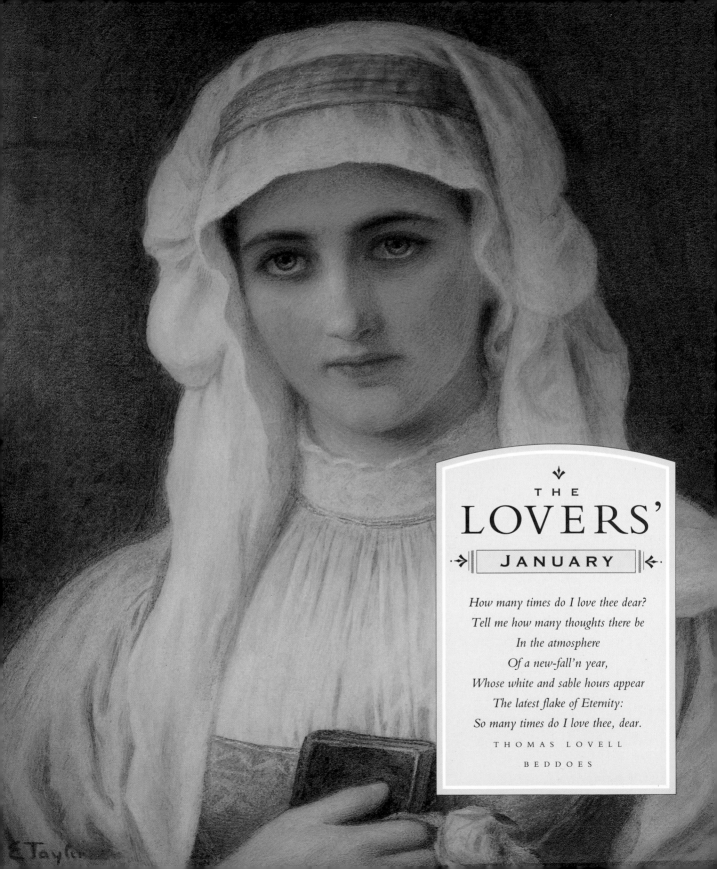

# THE
# LOVERS'
## JANUARY

*How many times do I love thee dear?*
*Tell me how many thoughts there be*
*In the atmosphere*
*Of a new-fall'n year,*
*Whose white and sable hours appear*
*The latest flake of Eternity:*
*So many times do I love thee, dear.*

THOMAS LOVELL

BEDDOES

# JANUARY

1

2

3

4

5

6

7

NOTES

*We are not the same persons this year as last; nor are those we love. It is a happy chance if we, changing, continue to love a changed person.*

W. SOMERSET MAUGHAM

LEFT: *Girl in a White and Gold Headscarf,* EDWARD TAYLOR (1828-1906)

# JANUARY

*Ask me no more, my*
*truth to prove,*
*What I would suffer for my love.*
*With thee I would in exile go*
*To regions of eternal snow,*
*O'er floods by solid ice confined,*
*Through forest bare with*
*northern wind . . .*

ELIZABETH TOLLET

8

9

10

11

12

13

14

NOTES

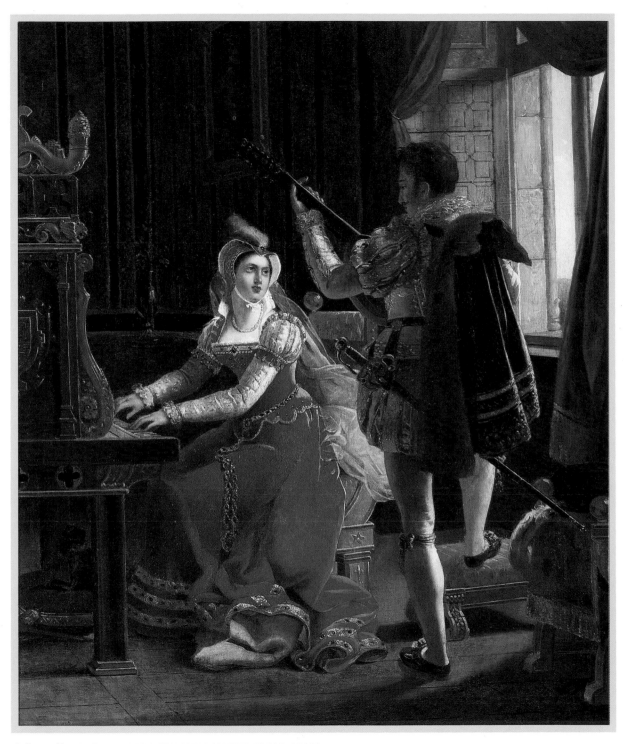

*A Love Duet*, FREDERICK WILLIAM HAYES (1848–1918)

> *Doubt that the stars are fire;*
> *Doubt that the sun*
> *doth move;*
> *Doubt truth to be a liar;*
> *But never doubt I love.*
>
> WILLIAM
> SHAKESPEARE

15

16

17

18

## ST AGNES' EVE

*St Agnes is the protector of virgins and was put to death for refusing to marry a man she did not love. On St Agnes' Eve, a girl can divine who her husband will be by baking a 'dumb' cake.*

Make a mixture of eggs, flour, water and salt into a cake, remaining dumb and fasting during the preparation. Mark with your initials and put the cake on the coals of a fire, to cook slowly through the night, first reciting:

*Sweet St Agnes, work thy fast*
*If ever I be to marry man,*
*Or ever man to marry me*
*I hope him this night to see.*

At midnight the spirit of the girl's future partner will turn the cake for her and prick his initials on it next to hers.

# JANUARY

_____

19

_____

20

_____

21

_____

NOTES

_____

*I have learned not to worry about love; but to honour its coming with all my heart.*
ALICE WALKER

*Feeding the Birds,* VINCENTA DE PARADES (1870–1910)

*The Gallant Skater*, FREDERICK HENDRICK KAEMMERER (1839-1902)

# JANUARY

22

23

24

25

26

27

28

NOTES

*'Tis that delightsome transport*
  *we can feel*
*Which painters cannot paint,*
*Nor words reveal,*
*Nor any art we know*
  *of can conceal.*

THOMAS PAINE

*If you tame me, then we shall need each other. To me, you will be unique in all the world. To you, I shall be unique in all the world.*

ANTOINE DE
SAINT-EXUPÉRY

29

30

31

NOTES

NOTES

NOTES

NOTES

NOTES

*The Bridal Sleigh Leaving a Snowbound Village,* ALFRED VON WIERUSZ KOWALSKI (1849-1915)

# THE
# LOVERS'
### ❖ FEBRUARY ❖

*I feed a flame within, which so torments me*
*That it both pains my heart, and*
*yet contents me:*
*'Tis such a pleasing smart, and I so love it,*
*That I had rather die than once remove it.*
*Yet he for whom I grieve shall*
*never know it;*
*My tongue does not betray, nor*
*my eyes show it.*
*Not a sigh, nor a tear, my pain discloses,*
*But they fall silently, like dew on roses.*

JOHN DRYDEN

# FEBRUARY

_____ 1 _____

_____ 2 _____

_____ 3 _____

_____ 4 _____

_____ 5 _____

_____ 6 _____

_____ 7 _____

NOTES

_____

*The best and most beautiful things in the world cannot be seen or even touched. They must be felt with the heart.*

HELEN KELLER

LEFT: *The Kiss*, FRANCESCO HAYEZ (1791–1881)

# FEBRUARY

*Go lovely Rose*
*Tell her that wastes her*
  *time and me,*
*That now she knows*
*When I resemble her to thee*
*How sweet she seems to be . . .*

EDMUND WALLER

8

9

10

11

12

13

14

NOTES

*King Rene's Honeymoon*, DANTE GABRIEL ROSSETTI (1828-1882)

## FEBRUARY

*I never saw so sweet a face*
*As that I stood before:*
*My heart has left its*
*dwelling-place*
*And can return no more.*

JOHN CLARE

*15*

*16*

*17*

*18*

*19*

*20*

*21*

NOTES

*Love makes a subtle man out of a crude one, it gives eloquence to the mute, it gives courage to the cowardly and makes the idle quick and sharp.*

JUAN RUIZ

*Lady and Prince Wrapped in Quilt,* INDIAN PAINTING (c1800)

*Hearts Are Trumps*, GEORGE EDWIN KILBURNE (1839-1924)

# FEBRUARY

_____ 22 _____

_____ 23 _____

> *Who hath not owned,*
> *with rapture-smitten frame,*
> *The power of grace, the magic*
> *of a name?*
>
> THOMAS CAMPBELL

_____ 24 _____

_____ 25 _____

_____ 26 _____

_____ 27 _____

_____ 28 _____

_____ 29 _____

# THE
# LOVERS'
## MARCH

*It is the first mild day of March*
*Each minute sweeter than before,*
*The redbreast sings from the tall larch*
*That stands beside our door.*
*There is a blessing in the air,*
*Which seems a sense of joy to yield*
*To the bare trees, and mountains bare,*
*And grass in the green field.*
*Love, now a universal birth,*
*From heart to heart is stealing,*
*From earth to man, from man to earth:*
*It is the hour of feeling.*

WILLIAM WORDSWORTH

# MARCH

1

2

3

4

5

6

7

NOTES

*When one loves somebody,*
*everything is clear - where to go,*
*what to do - it all takes care of*
*itself and one doesn't have to ask*
*anybody about anything.*

MAXIM GORKY

LEFT: *By The Sea,* CHARLES GREEN (1840-1898)

# MARCH

8

9

10

11

12

13

14

NOTES

*A Romantic Interlude*, HENRY ANDREWS (1830–1860)

*The Gamekeeper's Courtship*, GEORGE BERNARD O'NEILL (1828–1917)

# MARCH

_____

———— 15 ————

_____

———— 16 ————

_____

———— 17 ————

_____

———— 18 ————

_____

———— 19 ————

_____

———— 20 ————

_____

———— 21 ————

_____

NOTES

_____

_____

*My true love hath my heart,*
*and I have his,*
*By just exchange one for*
*another given:*
*I hold his dear, and mine he*
*cannot miss,*
*There never was a better*
*bargain driven:*
*My true love hath my heart,*
*and I have his.*

SIR PHILIP SIDNEY

# MARCH

22

23

24

25

———————————— ◆ ————————————
*26*

———————————— ◆ ————————————
*27*

———————————— ◆ ————————————
*28*

———————————— ◆ ————————————
NOTES

———————————— ◆ ————————————

*Anthea bade me tye her shoe;*
*I did; and kist the instep too;*
*And would have kist unto*
*her knee,*
*Had not her blush rebuked me.*
ROBERT HERRICK

## THE VIOLET OF VENUS

*The great lover Napoleon adopted the tiny violet as the emblem of his Imperial*
*Napoleonic Party. If picked in the last quarter of the moon, these tiny blooms are*
*said to have love-provoking powers. To make your love still sweeter, prepare a*
*violet sorbet by mixing together the following:*

*1 white of egg*
*2 tablespoons of lime juice*
*300ml/1 cup of grape juice*
*50g/2oz caster sugar/superfine sugar*
*200ml/$^1$/$_2$ cup sugar syrup*
*4 tablespoons of crème de*
*violette*

Put the egg white and caster
sugar to one side, mix the rest of
the ingredients together and
freeze until mushy. Then beat the
egg white and fold in the caster
sugar. Add all the mixture
together and freeze. Serve topped
with a few fresh violet flowers.

# MARCH

29

30

31

NOTES

NOTES

NOTES

NOTES

NOTES

> *We must resemble
> each other a little in order to
> understand each other, but we
> must be a little different to
> love each other.*
>
> PAUL GÉRALDY

*Psyche Carried off by Zephyr,* EGISTO FERRONI (1835-1912)

# THE
# LOVERS'
### APRIL

*Suddenly the window of my heart flew
open this morning, the window
that looks out on your heart.
I wondered to see that the name by
which you know me is written
in April leaves and flowers,
and I sat silent.*

RABINDRANATH TAGORE

# APRIL

1

2

3

4

5

6

7

NOTES

*If thou remember'st
not the slightest folly
That ever love did make
thee run into,
Thou hast not loved.*

WILLIAM
SHAKESPEARE

LEFT: *Through the White Flowers*, KATE GREENAWAY (1846-1901)

*Lover Telling of Love to Lady*, CHRISTINE DE PISIAN (Mid 15th Century)

# APRIL

8

9

10

11

12

13

14

*Nature, in giving tears to man, confessed that he Had a tender heart; this is our noblest quality.*

DECIMUS JUNIUS JUVENAL

NOTES

# APRIL

_15_

_16_

_17_

_18_

_19_

_20_

_21_

NOTES

*Sweet is the smile of home;*
*the mutual look,*
*When hearts are of each*
*other sure.*

JOHN KEBLE

*A Pensive Mood,* CHARLES SILLEM LIDDERDALE (1831–1895)

22

23

24

25

## A LOVER'S SPELL

*To enhance love, this spell can be done by two lovers together.*

Cut twelve hearts out of deep red coloured paper. Write your lover's name on six of the hearts and at the same time ask your lover to write his or her name on the other six.

Lay down a small mirror face up and put the hearts round it, alternating the name of your lover with your own. Light a red candle to rekindle passion and look down into the mirror, repeating your lover's name six times. Each time you do this, pick up one of the hearts with your lover's name on.

Take it in turns to sew one of the hearts to another with red thread. When all the hearts are sewn together, put them in a place where you want your love together to thrive.

# APRIL

---
*26*

---
*27*

---
*28*

---
NOTES

---

*Ask me why I send you here*
*This sweet infanta of the year?*
*Ask me why I send to you*
*This primrose, thus bepearl'd*
*with dew?*
*I will whisper to your ears:*
*The sweets of love are mix'd*
*with tears.*

ROBERT HERRICK

# APRIL

*If I had but two little wings*
*And were a little*
*feathery bird,*
*To you I'd fly, my dear!*
*But thoughts like these are*
*idle things,*
*And I stay here*

SAMUEL TAYLOR
COLERIDGE

29

30

NOTES

NOTES

NOTES

NOTES

NOTES

NOTES

You that think Love
  can convey No other way
But through the eyes,
  into the heart, His fatal dart,
Close up those casements,
  and but hear This syren sing;
And on the wing
Of her sweet voice it
  shall appear
That Love can enter
through the ear.

THOMAS CAREW

*A Man and a Woman at a Casement*, FRA FILIPPO LIPPI (1406–1469)

# THE LOVERS'

## MAY

She was a phantom of delight
When first she gleamed upon my sight;
A lovely apparition sent
To be a moment's ornament;
Her eyes as stars of twilight fair;
Like twilight's, too, her dusky hair;
But all things else about her drawn
From May-time and the cheerful dawn;
A dancing shape, an image gay,
To haunt, to startle, and waylay.

WILLIAM WORDSWORTH

## MAY

1

2

3

4

5

6

7

NOTES

*All love at first, like
generous wine,
Ferments and frets, until
'tis fine . . .*

SAMUEL BUTLER

LEFT: *Gathering Wild Flowers*, ALFRED GLENDENING (JNR) (1861–1907)

# MAY

8

9

10

11

## MAY

———— ✦ ————
*12*

———— ✦ ————
*13*

———— ✦ ————
*14*

———— ✦ ————
NOTES

———— ✦ ————

*And if Fate remember later, and
    come to claim her due,
What sorrow will be greater than
    the Joy I had with you?
For today, lit by your laughter,
    between the crushing years,
I will chance, in the hereafter,
    eternities of tears.*

LAWRENCE HOPE

> *Hard is the heart that loveth*
> *nought in May.*
> GEOFFREY CHAUCER

15

16

17

18

19

20

21

NOTES

*Reading a Book,* EDWARD TAYLER (1828-1906)

*By the Window,* JOHN SIMMONS (Fl. 1850)

## MAY

22

23

*Familiar acts are beautiful
through love.*

PERCY BYSSHE SHELLEY

24

25

26

27

28

NOTES

# MAY

_29_

_30_

_31_

NOTES

NOTES

NOTES

NOTES

NOTES

*Sweet, let us love enjoy,*
*And play and tick and toy,*
*And all our cares will drown;*
*Smile, laugh, and*
  *sometimes frown,*
*Make love's parenthesis*
*With a sweet, melting kiss.*
WILLIAM CAVENDISH

*Alain Chartier,* EDMUND BLAIR LEIGHTON (1903–1922)

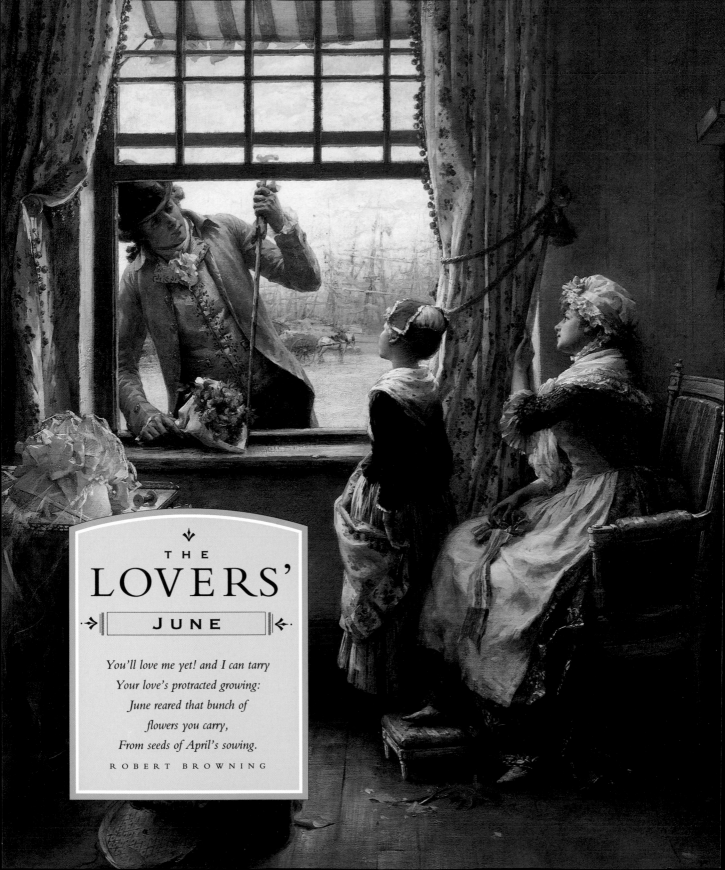

# THE
# LOVERS'
## JUNE

*You'll love me yet! and I can tarry*
*Your love's protracted growing:*
*June reared that bunch of*
*flowers you carry,*
*From seeds of April's sowing.*

ROBERT BROWNING

## JUNE

1

2

3

4

5

6

7

NOTES

*O my Luve's like a
red, red rose,
That's newly sprung in June;
O my Luve's like the melodie
That's sweetly play'd
in tune.*

ROBERT BURNS

LEFT: *A Secret Admirer,* PIERRE OUTIN (1840-1899)

## JUNE

_____8_____

_____9_____

A thing of beauty is a
  joy for ever:
Its loveliness increases; it
  will never
Pass into nothingness; but
  still will keep
A bower quiet for us,
  and a sleep
Full of sweet dreams, and
  health, and quiet breathing . . .

JOHN KEATS

_____10_____

_____11_____

_____12_____

_____13_____

_____14_____

NOTES

*Sweethearts*, FREDERICK MORGAN (1856–1927)

*Fete Champetre,* JOHN MASEY WRIGHT OWS (1777-1866)

# JUNE

_____

15

_____

16

_____

17

_____

18

_____

19

_____

20

_____

21

_____

NOTES

_____

> *I did but look and*
> *love awhile,*
> *'Twas but for one half-hour;*
> *Then to resist I had no will,*
> *And now I have no power.*
>
> THOMAS OTWAY

22

23

24

25

## THE PRETTY PANSY

*The pretty pansy was said to have been painted purple by one of cupid's arrows. As a bringer of kind thoughts and love, it is also called heart's ease; an infusion of pansy petals will cure a broken-hearted lover of all pain. Puck mischievously used an infusion of pansies to create chaos in* A Midsummer Night's Dream:

Yet markt I where the bolt of
  Cupid fell:
It fell upon a little western flower.
Before milk-white, now purple
  with love's wound,
And maidens call it love-in-idleness.

Fetch me that flower; the herb I
  shew'd thee once:
The juice of it on sleeping eyelids laid
Will make man or woman madly dote
Upon the next live creature
  that it sees.

WILLIAM SHAKESPEARE

# JUNE

---

26

---

27

---

28

---

NOTES

---

*Love has no other desire
but to fulfil itself. To melt and to
be like a running brook that
sings its melody to the night.
To wake at dawn with a winged
heart and give thanks for another
day of loving.*

KAHLIL GIBRAN

# J U N E

_I love thee and I love thee not,_

_I love thee, yet I'd rather not,_

_All of thee, yet I know_

_not what . . ._

THOMAS LOVELL
BEDDOES

---
29

---
30

---
N O T E S

---
N O T E S

---
N O T E S

---
N O T E S

---
N O T E S

---
N O T E S

---

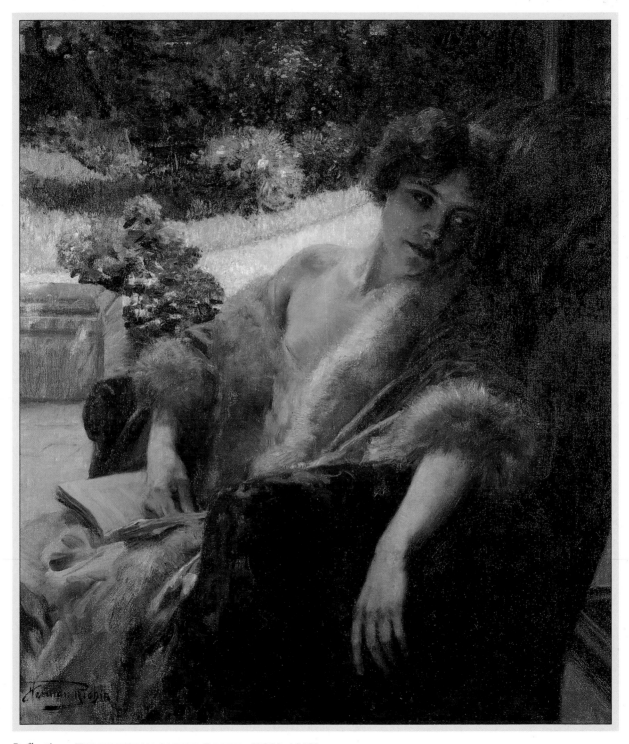

*Reflection*, HERMAN JEAN JOSEPH RICHIR (1866-1942)

# THE
# LOVERS'
## JULY

*Shall I compare thee to a summer's day?*
*Thou art more lovely and more temperate:*
*Rough winds do shake the*
*darling buds of May,*
*And summer's lease hath all*
*too short a date:*
*Sometime too hot the eye*
*of heaven shines,*
*And often is his gold complexion dimm'd;*
*And every fair from fair*
*sometimes declines,*
*By chance, or nature's changing*
*course, untrimm'd;*
*But thy eternal summer shall not fade . . .*

WILLIAM SHAKESPEARE

# J U L Y

———— 1 ————

———— 2 ————

———— 3 ————

———— 4 ————

———— 5 ————

———— 6 ————

———— 7 ————

N O T E S

*A life without love, without the presence of the beloved, is nothing but a mere magic-lantern show. We draw out slide after slide, swiftly tiring of each, and pushing it back to make haste for the next.*

J O H A N N   W O L F G A N G
G O E T H E

LEFT: *The Flirtatious Fisherman*, EDWIN THOMAS ROBERTS (1840-1917)

*Signing the Register*, JAMES CHARLES (1851–1906)

# JULY

_____

8

_____

9

*Never love unless you can*
*Bear with all the faults of man:*
*Men will sometimes jealous be,*
*Though but little cause they see;*
*And hang the head, as discontent,*
*And speak what straight they*
*  will repent.*

THOMAS CAMPION

_____

10

_____

11

_____

12

_____

13

_____

14

_____

NOTES

_____

*15*

*16*

*17*

*18*

## DRUID'S DRAUGHT

*In the heat of the summer, try sipping a refreshing Druid draught of immortality.
Take no more than a silver tablespoonful of this powerful love potion at sunset
and sunrise for seven days.*

Make an infusion of heather, honeysuckle, red clover and vervain steeped in around 300ml of pure spring water. Strain the mixture carefully before sipping.

Vervain is one of the Druid's seven sacred herbs, often called upon by witches and magicians to aid seduction plans and act as a cunning aphrodisiac.

## JULY

19

20

21

22

*Never seek to tell thy love,*
*Love that never told can be;*
*For the gentle wind doth move*
*Silently, invisibly.*
*I told my love, I told my love,*
*I told her all my heart,*
*Trembling, cold in ghastly fears.*
*All! She did depart!*
*A traveller came by,*
*Silently, invisibly:*
*He took her with a sigh.*

WILLIAM BLAKE

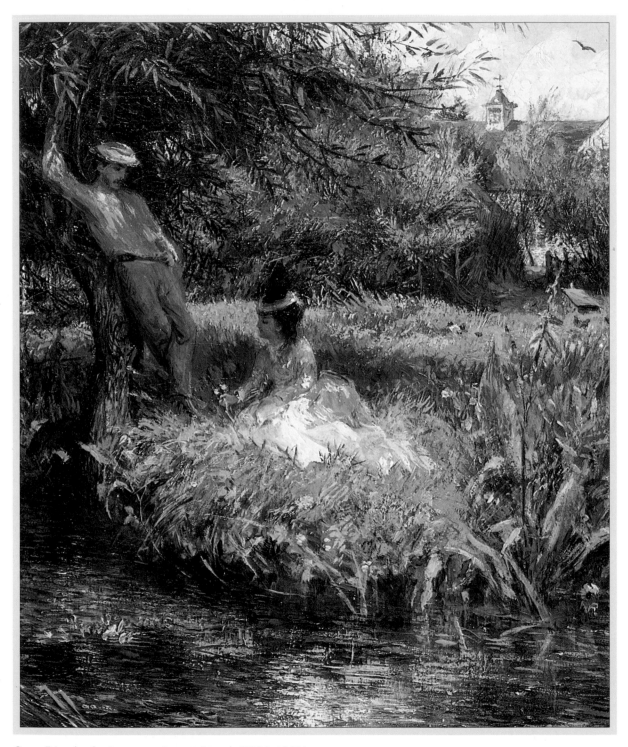

*On a Riverbank,* CHARLES JAMES LEWIS (1830-1892)

## JULY

_22_

_23_

_24_

_25_

_26_

_27_

_28_

N O T E S

_Two things cannot alter,_
_Since time was, nor today_
_The flowing of water;_
_And love's strange, sweet way._

## JULY

_____

29

_____

30

_____

31

*Be still, sad heart and*
*cease repining;*
*Behind the clouds is the sun*
*still shining;*
*Thy fate is the common*
*fate of all,*
*Into each life some rain*
*must fall.*

HENRY WADSWORTH
LONGFELLOW

*The Rose Bearer*, EDWARD KILLINGWORTH JOHNSON (1825–1923)

# THE
# LOVERS'

## AUGUST

*The fountains mingle with the river*
*And the rivers with the ocean,*
*The winds of heaven mix for ever*
*With a sweet emotion;*
*Nothing in the world is single;*
*All things by a law divine*
*In one spirit meet and mingle*
*Why not I with thine?*

PERCY BYSSHE SHELLEY

# AUGUST

———— 1 ————

———— 2 ————

———— 3 ————

———— 4 ————

———— 5 ————

———— 6 ————

———— 7 ————

NOTES

*To get the full value of joy,*
*you must have someone to*
*divide it with.*

MARK TWAIN

LEFT: *The Lover Surprised,* F J SCHALL (1752-1825)

# AUGUST

8

9

10

11

12

13

14

*Love, as told by the
seers of old,
Comes as a butterfly tipped
with gold,
Flutters and flies in
sunlit skies,
Weaving round hearts that
were one time cold.*

ALGERNON
SWINBURNE

NOTES

*Girl with a Butterfly*, HAROLD PIFFARD (1868–1939)

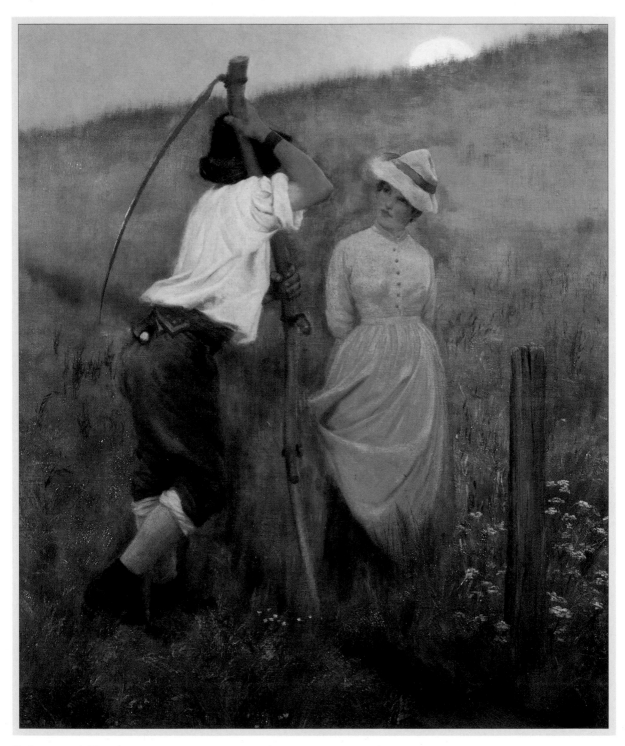

*Unfrequented Ways*, WILLIAM HENRY GORE (1880-1920)

# AUGUST

15

16

17

18

19

20

21

NOTES

Come away! Come sweet Love!
The golden morning wastes,
While the sun, from his sphere,
His fiery arrows casts,
Making all the shadows fly,
Playing, staying, in the grove
To entertain the stealth of love.
Thither, sweet Love, let us hie,
Flying, dying, in desire,
Winged with sweet hopes and
heavenly fire.

ANON

22

23

24

25

## THE FAIRY FLOWER

*The honeysuckle is said to be a flower of the fairies, its intoxicating scent strongest at nightfall.*

A young man could encourage a girl to dream passionately about him by repeating his name three times over a posy made of honeysuckle. He then had to steal into her room, in order to place the posy near her bed, so that as she slept she would breathe in the heady scent.

*Come to me in the silence of
  the night;
Come in the speaking silence
  of a dream;
Come with soft rounded cheeks
  and eyes as bright
As sunlight on a stream . . .*

CHRISTINA ROSSETTI

# AUGUST

---

26

---

27

---

28

---

NOTES

---

# AUGUST

———————————————— 29 ————————————————

———————————————— 30 ————————————————

———————————————— 31 ————————————————

*As perfume doth remain*
*In the folds where it hath lain,*
*So the thought of you, remaining*
*Deeply folded in my brain,*
*Will not leave me:*
*all things leave me:*
*You remain.*

ARTHUR SYMONS

NOTES

NOTES

NOTES

NOTES

NOTES

*Leisure Moments*, ERNEST WALBOURN (1897–1920)

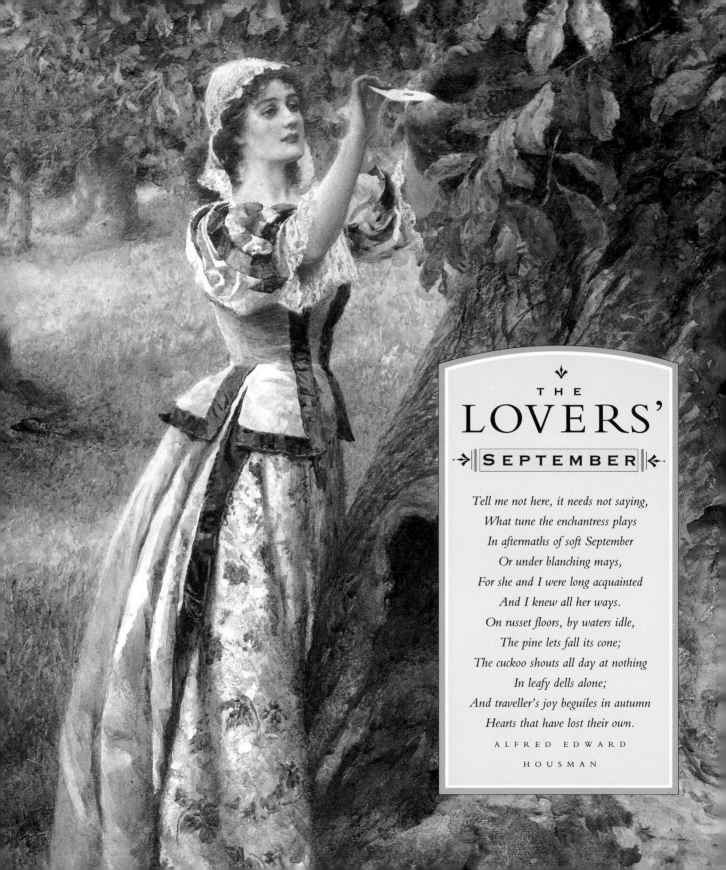

# THE LOVERS'
## ❧ SEPTEMBER ☙

Tell me not here, it needs not saying,
What tune the enchantress plays
In aftermaths of soft September
Or under blanching mays,
For she and I were long acquainted
And I knew all her ways.
On russet floors, by waters idle,
The pine lets fall its cone;
The cuckoo shouts all day at nothing
In leafy dells alone;
And traveller's joy beguiles in autumn
Hearts that have lost their own.

ALFRED  EDWARD
HOUSMAN

# SEPTEMBER

1

2

3

4

5

6

7

NOTES

*Love seeketh not itself to please*
*Nor for itself hath any care,*
*But for another gives its ease,*
*And builds a heaven in*
*hell's despair.*

WILLIAM BLAKE

LEFT: *Love's Letter Box*, ARTHUR HOPKINS (1848–1930)

*The Alarm*, JEAN FRANCOIS DETROY (1679-1752)

# SEPTEMBER

8

9

10

11

12

13

14

*What fortitude the soul*
*contains,*
*That it can so endure,*
*The accent of a coming foot,*
*The opening of a door!*
EMILY DICKINSON

NOTES

## SEPTEMBER

---
### 15
---
### 16
---
### 17
---
### 18
---

## A WINGED RETURN

A straying lover could be brought
back to the straight and narrow
by using a gypsy spell. A woman
wanting a man to return first had
to find the winged seeds of an ash
and an oak branch with an acorn.
In the myths of some lands the
ash tree actually created the first
man on earth, so it is a powerful
tree to use for calling love. This
charm should then be repeated
three nights in a row, while the
ash and oak are tucked under the
woman's pillow:

*Acorn cup and ashen key,*
*Bid my true love come to me -*
*Between moonlight and firelight,*
*Bring him over the hills tonight;*
*Over the meadows, over the moor,*
*Over the rivers, over the sea,*
*Over the threshold and in*
*  at the door.*
*Acorn cup and ashen key,*
*Bring my true love back to me.*

# SEPTEMBER

---

*19*

---

*20*

---

*21*

---

NOTES

---

*The Lovers*, SILVESTRO LEGA (1826–1895)

# SEPTEMBER

22

*Love reckons hours for
months, and days for years;
And every little absence
is an age.*

JOHN DRYDEN

23

24

25

26

27

28

NOTES

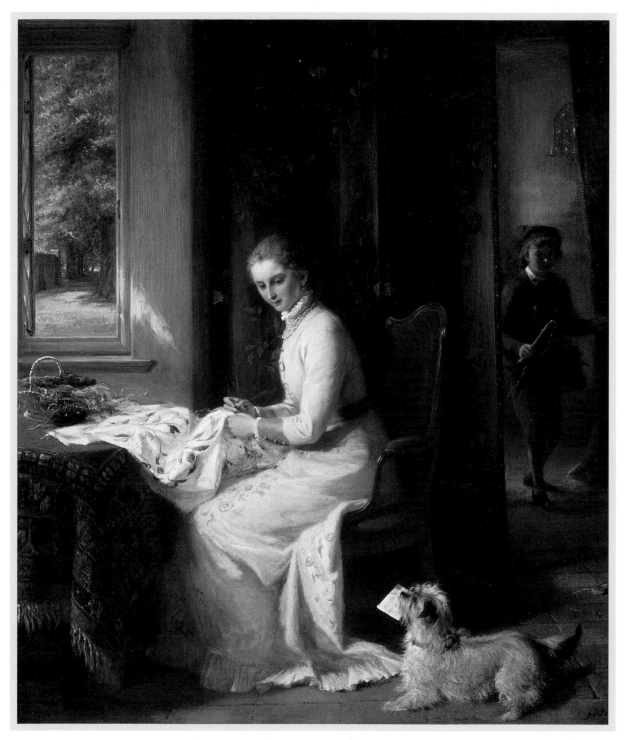

*The Love Letter*, GEORGE BERNARD O'NEILL (1828–1917)

*Lovers*, SZINYEI MERSE PAL (1879)

# SEPTEMBER

---
*29*

---
*30*

---
N O T E S

---
N O T E S

---
N O T E S

---
N O T E S

---
N O T E S

---
N O T E S

---

*Like mine own dear harp is*
*this my heart*
*Dumb, without the hand that*
*sweeps its strings;*
*Though the hand be careless*
*or be cruel,*
*When it comes, my heart breaks*
*forth and sings.*

SARAH WILLIAMS

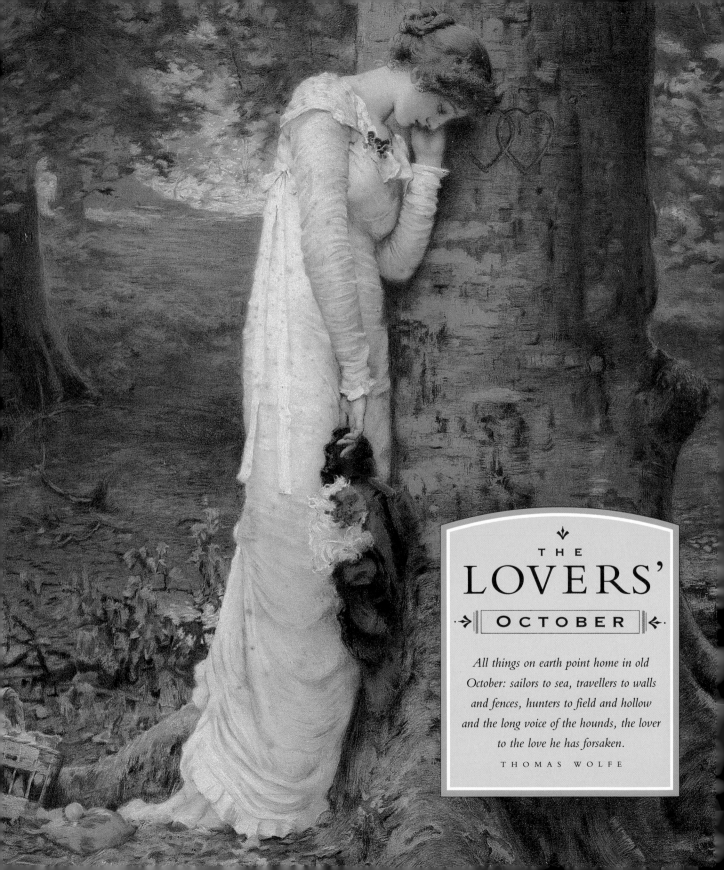

# THE
# LOVERS'

## OCTOBER

*All things on earth point home in old
October: sailors to sea, travellers to walls
and fences, hunters to field and hollow
and the long voice of the hounds, the lover
to the love he has forsaken.*

THOMAS WOLFE

# OCTOBER

—————————— ✦ ——————————
### 1

—————————— ✦ ——————————
### 2

—————————— ✦ ——————————
### 3

—————————— ✦ ——————————
### 4

—————————— ✦ ——————————
### 5

—————————— ✦ ——————————
### 6

—————————— ✦ ——————————
### 7

—————————— ✦ ——————————
NOTES

*Remember me when I am
gone away,
Gone far away into the
silent land;
When you can no more hold me
by the hand,
Nor I half turn to go, yet
turning stay,
Remember me when no more,
day by day,
You tell me of our future that
you plann'd:
Only remember me: you
understand
It will be too late to counsel
then or pray.*

CHRISTINA ROSSETTI

LEFT: *Absence Makes the Heart Grow Fonder,* MARCUS STONE (1840-1921)

## OCTOBER

8

9

10

*Love hath a language of*
*his own -*
*A voice that goes*
*From heart to heart - whose*
*mystic tone*
*Love only knows.*

THOMAS MOORE

11

12

13

14

NOTES

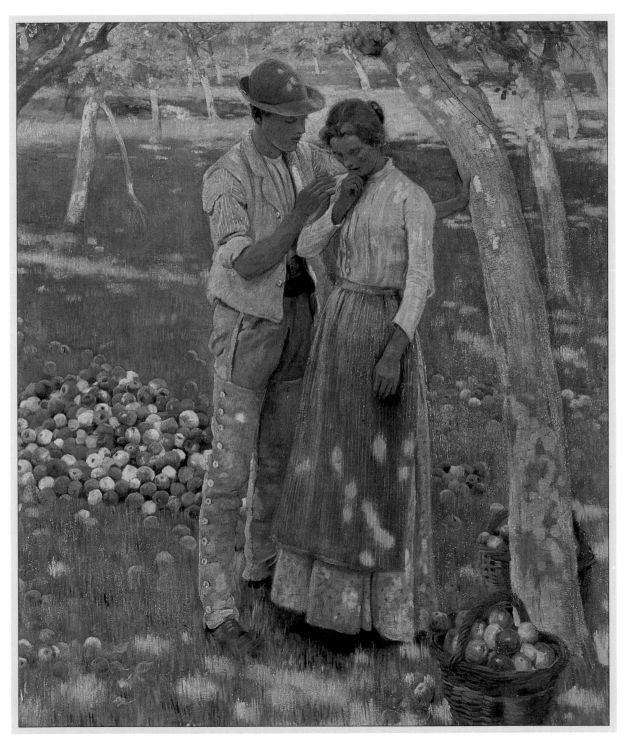

*The Orchard*, NELLY ERICHSEN (FL.1882–1897)

*The Lovers*, CESARE AUGUSTIN DETTI (1847–1914)

# OCTOBER

15

16

17

18

19

20

21

*For one human being to love
another; that is perhaps the most
difficult of all our tasks, the
ultimate, the last test and proof,
the work for which all other work
is but preparation.*

RAINER MARIA RILKE

NOTES

# OCTOBER

*There is no season when such pleasant and sunny spots may be lighted on, and produce so pleasant an effect on the feelings, as now in October.*

NATHANIEL
HAWTHORNE

22

23

24

25

*A Rustic Courtship*, THOMAS JAMES LLOYD (1849–1910)

# OCTOBER

---

*26*

---

*27*

---

*28*

---

NOTES

---

## HALLOWEEN HAZELS

*The supernatural powers of the magic hazel tree are called on in many games to test a lover's intentions.*

An engaged couple would select a hazelnut each and put them in the fire. If they jumped together in the heat their union would be successful but if one nut jumped out of the fire, that meant the owner would be unfaithful.

For a girl to find out if someone she admired shared her love, she would name the man, place the nut in the fire and demand:

*If you love me, pop and fly*
*If you hate me, burn and die.*

A nut that popped loudly, bursting, meant that the man was bursting with love for her, whilst a nut that did nothing meant there was no interest.

# OCTOBER

Why are thou silent! Is thy
love a plant
Of such weak fibre that the
treacherous air
Of absence withers what was
once so fair?

WILLIAM
WORDSWORTH

29

30

31

NOTES

NOTES

NOTES

NOTES

NOTES

# OCTOBER

*Faraway Thoughts,* ANON

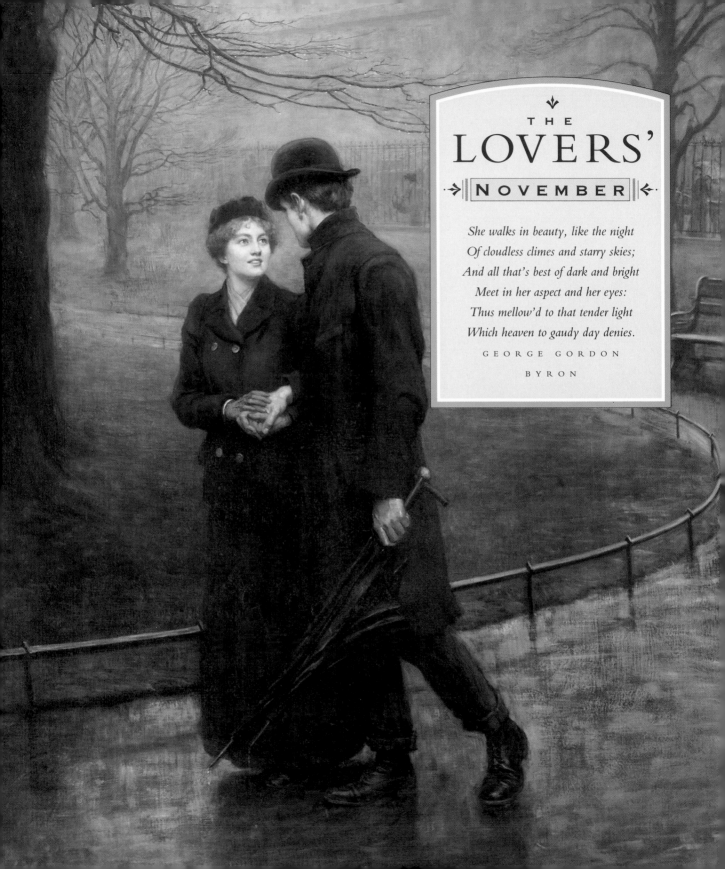

# THE LOVERS'
### ‣‣ NOVEMBER ‣‣

*She walks in beauty, like the night*
*Of cloudless climes and starry skies;*
*And all that's best of dark and bright*
*Meet in her aspect and her eyes:*
*Thus mellow'd to that tender light*
*Which heaven to gaudy day denies.*

GEORGE GORDON
BYRON

# NOVEMBER

_____ ◆ _____
1

_____ ◆ _____
2

_____ ◆ _____
3

_____ ◆ _____
4

*There is a smile of love,*
*And there is a smile of deceit,*
*And there is a smile of smiles*
*In which these two smiles meet.*

WILLIAM BLAKE

_____ ◆ _____
5

_____ ◆ _____
6

_____ ◆ _____
7

_____ ◆ _____
NOTES

_____ ◆ _____

LEFT: *The Garden of Eden*, HUGH GOLDWYN RIVIERE (1869–1947)

*The Introduction*, GEORGE GOODWIN KILBURNE (1839–1924)

# NOVEMBER

8

9

10

11

12

13

14

*To be loved at first sight, a man should have at the same time something to respect and something to pity in his face.*

STENDHAL

NOTES

_____

15

_____

16

_____

17

*Love rules the court, the*
*camp, the grove,*
*And men below, and*
*saints above;*
*For love is heaven, and*
*heaven is love.*

SIR WALTER SCOTT

_____

18

_____

19

_____

20

_____

21

_____

NOTES

_____

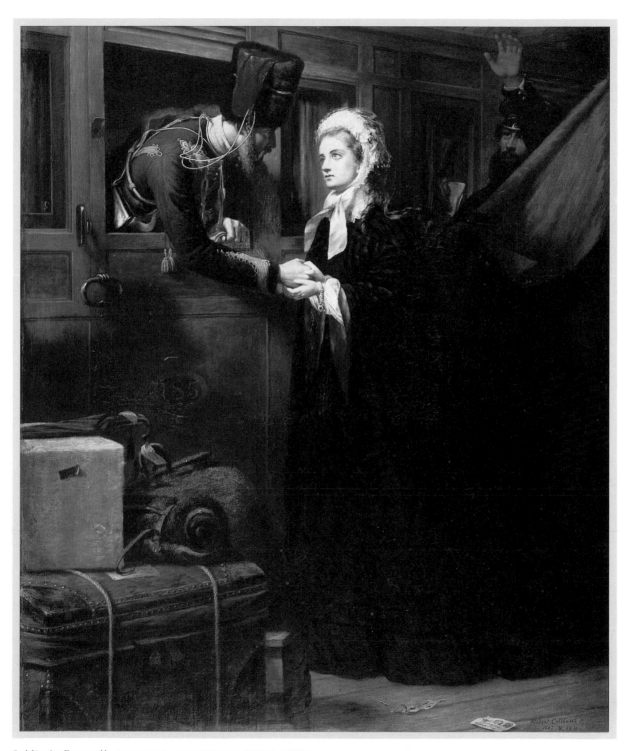

*Soldier's Farewell*, RICHARD COLLINSON (1832–1890)

22

23

24

25

### APPLE OF MY EYE

The apple has been considered an aphrodisiac ever since Eve tempted
Adam with it in the Garden of Eden. It is the sacred symbol of
love and protection in witchcraft. The juice of apples can be drunk to
attract love or improve prowess.

If an unmarried girl peels an apple in a continuous strip without
breaking it, she should then fling it over her left shoulder. If it falls
in one piece, the shape will indicate the initial of the man.

## NOVEMBER

26
_____

27
_____

28
_____

NOTES
_____

*We don't love qualities,*
*we love a person; sometimes by*
*reason of their defects as well as*
*their qualities.*

JACQUES MARITAIN

*The Tryst,* WILLIAM HOLYDAKE (1834–1894)

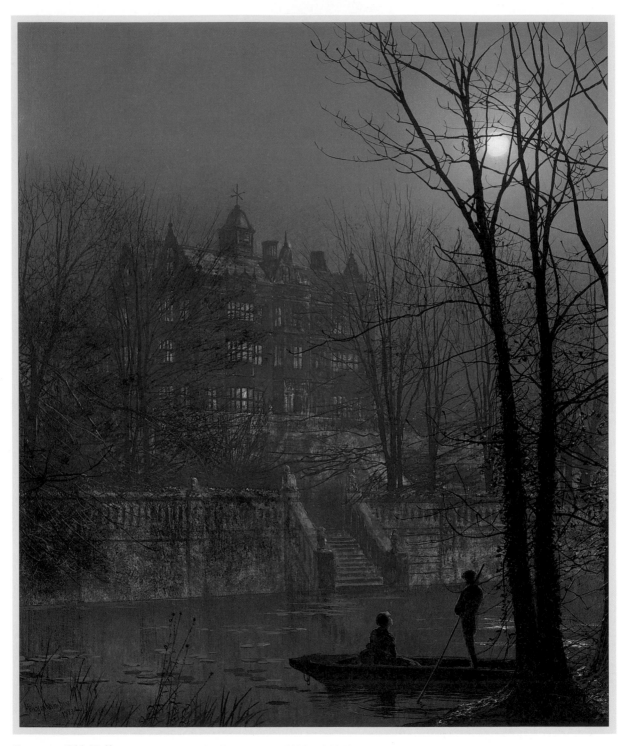

*Knostrop Old Hall*, JOHN ATKINSON GRIMSHAW (1836–1893)

# November

29

30

NOTES

NOTES

NOTES

NOTES

NOTES

NOTES

*The night is dark and your slumber is deep in the hush of my being. Wake, O Pain of Love, for I know not how to open the door, and I stand outside.*

RABINDRANATH
TAGORE

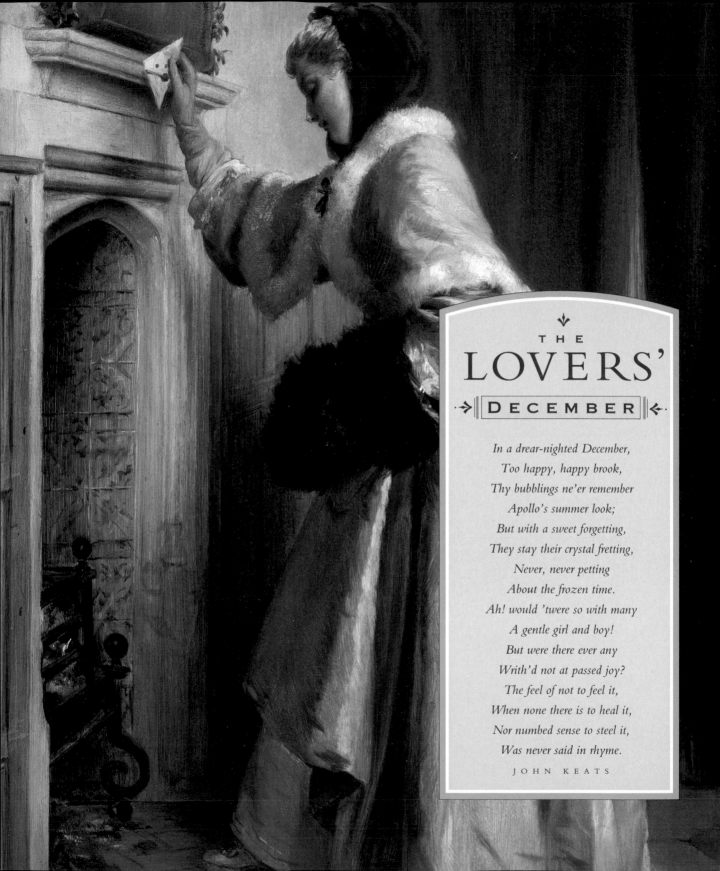

# THE
# LOVERS'
## ❖ DECEMBER ❖

In a drear-nighted December,
Too happy, happy brook,
Thy bubblings ne'er remember
Apollo's summer look;
But with a sweet forgetting,
They stay their crystal fretting,
Never, never petting
About the frozen time.
Ah! would 'twere so with many
A gentle girl and boy!
But were there ever any
Writh'd not at passed joy?
The feel of not to feel it,
When none there is to heal it,
Nor numbed sense to steel it,
Was never said in rhyme.

JOHN KEATS

# DECEMBER

1

2

3

4

5

6

7

NOTES

LEFT: *Madame Se Chauffe*, JOHN CALLCOTT HORSLEY (1817-1903)

# DECEMBER

> *Now all my days are trances,*
> *And all my nightly dreams*
> *Are where thy grey*
> *eye glances,*
> *And where thy footstep*
> *gleams -*
> *In what ethereal dances*
> *By what eternal streams!*
>
> EDGAR ALLAN POE

8

9

10

11

12

13

14

NOTES

*Under the Mistletoe*, EDWARD FREDERICK BREWTNALL (1846–1902)

---

*15*

---

*16*

---

*17*

---

*18*

---

### DECEMBER DELIGHT

The red rose is said to have a blush that came from the blood of
Aphrodite. While attempting to save her lover Adonis, from a wild boar,
she had to clamber through a white bush of briar roses. The blood from
the scratches on her feet stained the briar and gave the world the first
red roses. The red rose has been a lover's symbol ever since.

If a young girl wraps a red rose carefully in white tissue paper on
Midsummer's eve, she should put it away until Christmas.
If on Christmas day she finds it is still intact, she should wear it and
the first man to admire it will become her husband.

## DECEMBER

—————————— ❧ ——————————
### 19

—————————— ❧ ——————————
### 20

—————————— ❧ ——————————
### 21

—————————— ❧ ——————————
NOTES

—————————— ❧ ——————————

*Among those whom I like or admire, I can find no common denominator, but among those whom I love, I can: all of them make me laugh.*

WYSTAN HUGH AUDEN

*Going to a Christmas Party,*
GEORGE SHERIDAN KNOWLES (1863-1931)

*Christmas Shopping,* HAROLD PIFFARD (1895–1899)

# DECEMBER

22

23

24

*Love and Time with
  reverence use,
Treat them like a parting friend;
Nor the golden gifts refuse
Which in youth sincere
  they send:
For each year their price is more,
And less simple than before.*

JOHN DRYDEN

25

26

27

28

NOTES

# December

_____

*29*

_____

*30*

The heart has its reasons
which reason cannot know.
BLAISE PASCAL

_____

*31*

_____

NOTES

_____

NOTES

_____

NOTES

_____

NOTES

_____

NOTES

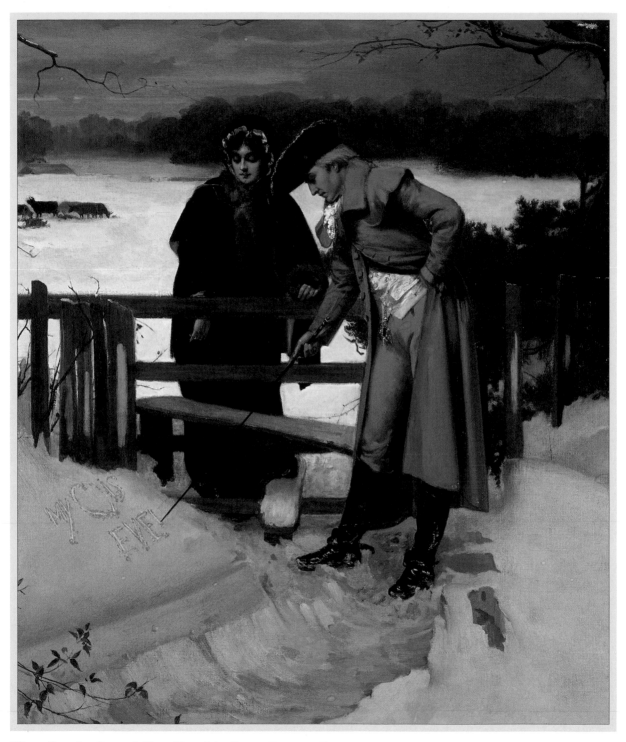

*'Twas Ever So, Lovers' Vows Traced in Snow*, WILLIAM HOLYDAKE (1834–1894)